Georgie
and the
Robbers

Stan Cullimore

Chapter one

Georgie Brown was born on 13 June 1956.
She had just had her eleventh birthday.

Georgie sat on her bed and looked at the red
moneybox in front of her. It was full of money.
Georgie began to count it.

Suddenly Georgie's mum put her head into
the room.

"Are you coming
down to the shops
with your dad and
me, Georgie?"

Georgie finished counting her money and looked up. She nodded.

"Yes. I want to go to the post office and pay this money in."

Georgie was saving up to buy herself a record player.

"Well, hurry up and get ready. We will be going in a minute."

Georgie stood up.

"I'm ready!"

A few minutes later Georgie set off with her mum and dad.

Chapter Two

Georgie stopped when they got to the post office.

"I'm going in here," she said.

She got ready to cross the road. She waited as a red car pulled up in front of her. It stopped right outside the post office.

"We will meet you in that café over there in ten minutes," said Dad.

"All right," said Georgie.

She crossed the road and walked round the red car. She saw that the wheels had got orange mud all over them.

As Georgie went past the car, two men got out. One was holding a big blue bag. They looked around slowly and then nodded to each other.

Georgie waved to her mum and dad as they walked away. She turned to go into the post office. But the two men from the car pushed past her and went in first.

"Watch it," said Georgie. "You almost pushed me over!"

But the men did not say a word to her.

Chapter Three

Inside the post office Georgie saw a long line of people. They were all waiting by the counter.

"Oh no," groaned Georgie. "I will be here for ages."

The two men who had pushed past Georgie were not in the line of people.

"I wonder where they went?" thought Georgie. She did not have to wait long to find out.

"OK. All of you, put your hands up," shouted a loud voice.

Georgie looked round. It was one of the men she had seen get out of the car. The man was holding something that looked very much like a gun.

"I've got a gun," said the man. "Do as you are told and you won't get hurt."

People started to put their hands in the air. Georgie did the same. Soon everyone had their hands up.

"That's good," said the man.

The other man that Georgie had seen was beside the counter. He opened his big blue bag.

"You," he shouted at the girl behind the counter. "Give me all the money. And no tricks or my friend over there will start shooting those people."

The girl looked very scared. She was shaking. She opened the money drawer beside her. Then she took out a big pile of notes.

"Hurry up," shouted the man.

The girl took out another big pile of notes and then another. Soon there was a lot of money on the counter.

"There, that's all of it," said the girl.

"Put it all in there," snapped the man.

He pointed at the big blue bag on the counter. The girl put all the money into the bag.

"Right, we're ready to go," said the man.

The man with the gun nodded.

"OK. Now listen to me all of you. Stay here and don't try to follow us or I will have to use this!"

The two men ran out of the post office with the bag.

Chapter Four

The post office was silent after the two men had gone. Then the manager went over to the counter.

"All right everybody," he said. "It's all right. The robbers have gone. I have called the police and they are on their way here now. So just stay calm."

Everyone started to talk at once.

Then the door burst open and four policemen ran in. They looked around.

"Where are they?" one of the policemen shouted.

"They've just left," said the manager.

The policemen raced out of the post office.

Georgie followed them outside.

One of the policemen was talking into a radio. Georgie walked up to one of the other policemen.

"I saw them get out of a car," she said.

The policemen nodded.

"Great. Can you tell me what sort of car it was?"

Georgie shook her head.

"No. But it was red and it had orange mud all over the wheels," she said. "And the men both had long brown hair."

The policeman looked really pleased.

"Well done, young lady. That is very useful. Can you wait here for a minute? Someone will have to write down what you saw."

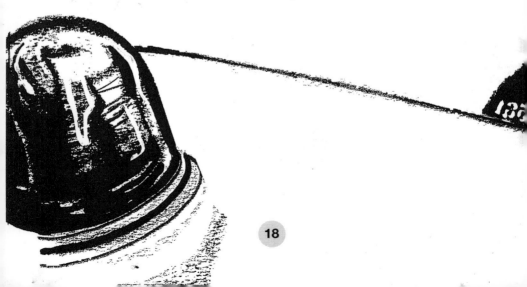

18

Another policeman came over to Georgie.

"I bet they will be miles away by now," he said. "But now we know what colour their car is, we know what to look for."

The two policemen started to talk to each other.

"I'd better go and tell my mum and dad about it all. But I'll be right back," said Georgie.

One of the policemen nodded.

"Good."

Georgie crossed the road and went into the café. Her mum and dad were having a cup of coffee. Georgie did not sit down at the table.

"Mum, Dad – the post office has just been robbed," she said.

Three men were sitting at the table next to Georgie's mum and dad. One of them turned to look at Georgie. Georgie had seen him before somewhere.

Chapter Five

Georgie told her mum and dad what had happened. She looked at the three men again. Suddenly she gasped. She knew where she had seen that man before. He had been driving the red car outside the post office. Georgie sat down.

"What are you doing, Georgie?" asked Mum.

"You have to go back so the police can write down what you saw," said Dad. "Come on!"

Mum and Dad stood up. Georgie tried to think.
She did not know what to do. She stood up
and looked around at the three men. She
shook her head. She must have been wrong.
The other two men had very short black hair.
They weren't the robbers. Georgie followed
her mum and dad out of the café.

Chapter Six

Outside the café, Georgie stopped. She had to be sure. She was just about to go back inside when she saw a car parked round the back of the café. It was red. Georgie went over to the car. She looked at the wheels.

"Wow," she gasped.

They were covered in orange mud.

Then she saw something on the back seat of
the car. It was a long brown wig! Georgie knew
what she had to do. She went back to her
mum and dad.

"Come on," she cried.

Chapter Seven

Five minutes later Georgie was back behind the café. But this time she had four policemen with her. She showed them the car and the wig. One of the policemen shook his head.

"These robbers are really clever," he said. "They knew we would be looking for them. And they knew we would think they were miles away. So they decided to stay right here!"

Then one of the other policemen turned to Georgie.

"You will have to show us where the men are," he said. "But be careful. They are armed!"

Georgie nodded.

Seconds later she walked into the café. She walked past the three men sitting at the table. She then bent down and began to tie her shoe lace. This was the sign the policemen had been waiting for. The door burst open and four policemen raced into the café.

They raced over to the three men.

"Put your hands up," shouted one of the policemen. "You are under arrest."

The three men put their hands up.

Chapter Eight

Some time later, when Georgie had finished talking to the police, the post office manager came up to her.

"So you are the girl who helped us catch the robbers, are you?"

Georgie nodded.

"We got all our money back, thanks to you. So I think you should get a reward."

He handed Georgie a five-pound note.

"Wow," Georgie gasped. "That's a lot of money. I can afford to buy myself a new record player now!"